WALT DISNEP'S
THREE LITTLE PIGS

retold by Barbara Brenner

Random House New York

Copyright © 1972 by The Walt Disney Company. • Lyrics for song "Who's Afraid of the Big Bad Wolf" Copyright 1933 BOURNE CO., New York, N.Y. Copyright Renewed • Used By Permission • All rights reserved under International and Pan-American Copyright Conventions. Published in the United States by Random House, Inc., New York, and simultaneously in Canada by Random House of Canada Limited, Toronto.

Library of Congress Cataloging in Publication Data
Brenner, Barbara.   The three little pigs.
Three little pigs leave home to seek their fortunes and have to deal with a wicked wolf.
[1. Folklore] I. The three little pigs. Motion picture II. Title
PZ10.3.B753Th   398.2'452'9734 [E] 72-5132   ISBN 0-394-82522-5
ISBN 0-394-92522-x (lib. bdg.)

Manufactured in the United States of America

F G H I
6 7 8 9

This is the story of three little pigs,
and one big, bad wolf.

The three little pigs lived in a house
at the bottom of a hill.
They lived with their mother.

The big, bad wolf lived in a house
at the top of the hill.
He lived alone.

One day Mother Pig said,
"Boys, it's time for you to go your own way.
And to live in your own houses."

"Yes, it is time," said the first little pig.
"To go our own way," said the second little pig.
"And to live in our own houses," said the
third little pig.
So the three little pigs packed their bags.
They left the house at the bottom of the hill.

"Good-by now," their mother said.

"And don't forget—watch out for the big, bad wolf.

He eats little pigs.

"We won't forget," said the three little pigs.

"B is for big," said the first little pig.

"B is for bad," said the second little pig.

"Wolf is for wolf," said the third little pig.

They waved good-by and went their merry way.

Soon they came to a place where three roads met.
"I'll go this way and build a house," said pig
number one.
"I'll go that way and build a house," said pig
number two.

"And I'll stay right here and build my house," said
pig number three.

So each little pig went his own way.

The first little pig built his house of straw.

One, two, three, snip, snap! His house was done.

It was not a very good house.

It was not a very strong house.

"But who cares?" said the little pig.
"I don't want to work all day.
I want to dance and play."
He did.

But *someone* was watching from the hill.
Someone who liked to eat little pigs.

The second little pig
built his house of sticks.
One, two, three, zip, zap!
His house was done.
It was not a very good house.
Or very strong.
"But who cares?" said that little pig.
"I don't want to work all day.
I want to sing and play."
This is what he did.

But *someone* was watching from the hill.
Someone who liked to eat little pigs.

The third little pig built his house of bricks.
Now this little pig worked hard.
He made a floor of wood.

He made a door.

He built his house brick by brick.
And he made a chimney on the roof.
When it was done, it was a good house.
And a strong house.

"Now I have time to rest and play,"
said the third little pig.
And so he did.

But *someone* was watching from the hill.
Someone who liked to eat little pigs.

Next day, *someone* came down the hill.

THE BIG, BAD, WOLF!

He went to the house of straw.

He banged on the door.

"Little pig, little pig, let me come in," he called.

The first little pig looked out the window.

He saw the big, bad wolf.

"No, no, by the hair of my chinny-chin-chin,
I won't let *you* in," said the little pig.

"Then I'll huff, and I'll puff, and I'll blow
your house in," said the wolf.

He huffed, and he puffed.
And he blew that house of straw right down!

The little pig got out just in time.

He ran to his brother's house of sticks.

"Help! Help!" he cried. "The big, bad wolf is coming."

The second little pig quickly let him in,

and locked the door.

Now the big, bad wolf put on a sheep's skin.

He went to the house of sticks.

He banged on the door.

"Little pigs, little pigs, let me come in," he said,

in a sweet voice.

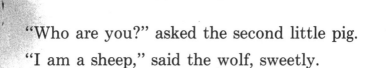

"Who are you?" asked the second little pig.
"I am a sheep," said the wolf, sweetly.

The two little pigs looked out the window.
They could see the wolf's eyes under the sheep's skin.
So the second little pig said,
"No, no, by the hair of my chinny-chin-chin.
I won't let you in."

"Then I'll huff, and I'll puff, and I'll blow
your house in," said the wolf.

He huffed, and he puffed.
And he huffed, and he puffed.

And he blew that house of sticks right down!

The two little pigs got out just in time.
They ran to their brother's house of bricks.

"Help! Help! The big, bad wolf is coming."

The third little pig quickly let them in,
and locked the door.

The wolf came. He began to bang on the door.
"Little pigs, little pigs, let me come in," the wolf called.
"No, no, by the hair of my chinny-chin-chin,
I won't let you in," said the third little pig.
"Then I'll huff, and I'll puff, and I'll blow
your house in," said the wolf.

The two little pigs were afraid.

But the third little pig said,

"Don't be afraid. The wolf can't blow this house in.

This is a very strong house."

He said to the wolf,
"Go ahead, blow. Blow your head off.
We're not afraid of a big, bad wolf."

So the wolf began. . . .

He huffed, and he puffed.
And he huffed, and he puffed.
Then he puffed, and huffed . . .
puff huff huff puff.

His face got red.

His ears got blue.

His eyes began

BUT . . .

he co

...ouse of bricks!

Now the wolf was mad!
He had to get those pigs.
"I know what I'll do," he said.

"I'll go up the side of the house—
brick by brick.

Then I'll slide down through the chimney."

The three little pigs heard him on the roof.

"He's on the roof," said pig number one.

"He'll come down the chimney," said pig number two.

Pig number three said, "Quick!
Get a pot of hot water."
They got a pot of hot water.

It was *very* hot!

They put it under the chimney.

The wolf came down the chimney.

PLOP! He fell right into the pot of hot water.

"Help! Help!" cried the wolf. "I'm in hot water!"

He jumped up.
He ran out of the house.
He ran, and ran, and did not stop
until he got to his house.
And he never came down the hill again.

The wolf still lives in his house,
at the top of the hill.
Alone.
He is still big, but he isn't so bad.
He never eats little pigs any more.

Now the three little pigs live together
in the house of bricks.
They play and sing and are merry all day long.

"Who's afraid of the big bad wolf,
The big bad wolf, the big bad wolf?
Who's afraid of the big bad wolf?
Tra la la la la-a-a-a!"